Willie Takes a Hike

Willie
Takes
a Hike

GLORIA RAND

ILLUSTRATED BY
TED RAND

Harcourt Brace & Company

San Diego   New York   London

Library of Congress Cataloging-in-Publication Data
Rand, Gloria
Willie takes a hike/by Gloria Rand;
illustrated by Ted Rand.—1st ed.
p. cm.
Summary: After moving to a new home at the junkyard,
Willie the mouse disobeys his parents, goes hiking by himself,
and gets lost in the unfamiliar surroundings.
ISBN 0-15-200272-3
[1. Mice—Fiction. 2. Hiking—Fiction. 3. Safety—Fiction.
4. Lost children—Fiction.] I. Rand, Ted, ill. II. Title.
PZ7.R1553Wi   1996
[E]—dc20   95-13698

First edition
A B C D E

Printed in Singapore

The illustrations in this book were drawn in indelible pen
and painted in watercolors and liquid dye on 100 percent rag stock.
The display type was set in Goudy Sans.
The text type was set in Minion.
Color separations by Bright Arts, Ltd., Singapore
Printed and bound by Tien Wah Press, Singapore
This book was printed with soya-based inks on Leykam recycled
paper, which contains more than 20 percent postconsumer waste and
has a total recycled content of at least 50 percent.
Production supervision by Warren Wallerstein and Cheryl Kennedy
Designed by Lydia D'moch

For all search-and-rescue volunteers,
who selflessly risk their own lives to aid others

—*G. R. and T. R.*

The day Willie and his parents moved from an apartment house into a junkyard at the edge of town, Willie wanted to take a hike.

"Not a good idea," his mother warned. "You haven't learned your way around. You might get lost."

"Besides, remember rule number one," his father added.

"I know. Never hike alone," Willie replied. "But who could I hike with? My friends are all back at the apartment. What if I just hike near our nest?"

"No," his parents answered.

"Can I pretend I'm hiking?" Willie asked hopefully.

"Now that would be fine, just pretend." Willie's mother sounded pleased and smiled as she unpacked and put things into cupboards, closets, and dresser drawers.

"Just pretend," his father agreed, as he stowed books up on high shelves.

Quickly Willie rummaged through boxes until he found his hiking boots and jacket. When he found his backpack he stuffed it with a sweater, a flashlight, and a bandanna, extras that hikers always take along. He added a plastic garbage bag— one he'd cut a hole in for his head—so it could be an instant raincoat. Then Willie packed cheese and crackers for lunch, raisins for a snack, and clipped a canteen full of water onto his belt.

"Better not forget this," Willie reminded himself as he hung a whistle around his neck. "Gotta have my whistle."

Then Willie set off on a trail through packing boxes and around furniture, until he came to the nest's front door.

What if I go only a little way? Willie asked himself. I won't go far. My folks are so busy they'll never notice.

When he was sure no one was looking, Willie left, quiet as a mouse, and scampered up onto a stack of crates. From this look-out he could see across the whole junkyard.

Without a backward glance, Willie
scurried over to a pile of pipe.

He slid down one of the pipes and
popped out by a bush loaded with beauti-
ful berries. They were tempting, but Willie
knew better. He'd been told over and over
never to eat berries unless his parents had
said they were safe to eat. Berries that
looked delicious might be poisonous.

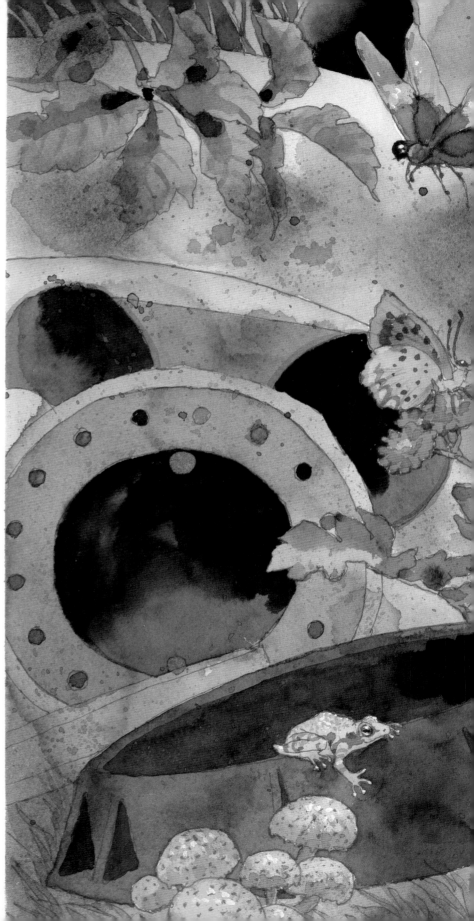

Willie was having so much fun hiking through the junk he completely forgot to stay near home. He didn't forget to eat his lunch, however. He picked a perfect place to have a picnic, right by a sparkling pond.

"Time to go wading," Willie said after lunch. "This nice cool water will make my feet feel good."

While he was putting his boots back on, he saw a snake slipping out from behind a cracked sink.

Willie knew that snakes eat mice whole. He hid up inside a rusty faucet.

"Better get back home," Willie whispered to himself, after the snake had gone on by. But just then he saw a collection of old windows and forgot about returning to the nest.

"Hey! It's me, the great hiker," he bragged as he paraded back and forth in front of the glass, admiring his own reflection. "It's me, the greatest hiker in the world."

Willie, the great hiker, decided to climb to the top of a huge coil of rope. Height was not the danger, though; the danger was directly below. A large raccoon had appeared, right where Willie had been marching.

"Too many enemies around here for me," Willie muttered.

He grabbed a vine and swung over to a row of oil drums. Uh-oh, more danger! On top of the drums, just where Willie needed to land, sat a big cat.

"Oh, no!" Willie screeched. "Not a cat!"

The cat swatted at Willie as he flew past to a mound of tires. Down through the tires he raced, getting far away from the cat as fast as possible. Round and round Willie ran, until he got so dizzy he couldn't stand up.

"I wish I was back home.
Wish I knew which way to go!"
Willie looked around. "I think
I'm in trouble. I think I'm lost!"
Willie began to cry.

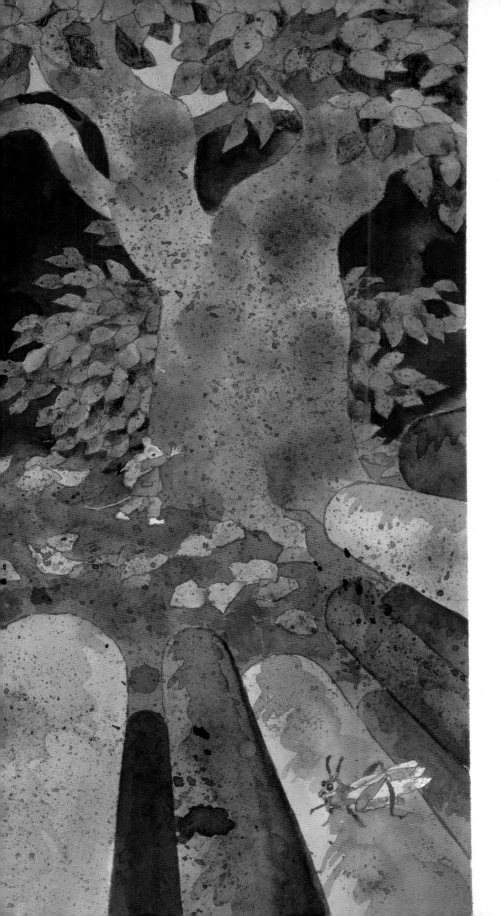

"Better do what I'm supposed to do," Willie finally decided. "I'm supposed to stop right where I first realize I don't know where I am, and I'm supposed to hug the nearest tree. A tree will be my friend while I wait to be found. I'm supposed to blow my whistle, too, so searchers can hear where I am."

Willie felt silly hugging a tree, but he was certain he had found a friend when he sat down close to its sturdy trunk. He blew his whistle over and over again, even though it's hard to blow a whistle when you're crying.

Late in the afternoon Willie realized he might not be found before dark. He might have to spend the night out in the wilderness. It was time to quit crying. There were things he needed to do.

Willie tied his bandanna onto a bush by the tree, a signal to searchers that he was close by. Then he made a bed of branches so he wouldn't have to sleep on the cold, damp ground and gathered leaves to cover himself so he'd stay warm. Willie was sure he was remembering all he should remember, and he began to feel very brave.

After a dinner of raisins, Willie put on his extra sweater and snuggled down.

An owl hooted high above Willie's bed and woke him up from a sound sleep. *Whoooo, whooo.* Willie stayed very quiet, hidden under his blanket of leaves, until the owl flew away.

Later, loud noises and crashing sounds woke him up again. But Willie stayed brave and shined his flashlight all around. No one was there. Sometimes small creatures sound big in the dark. It could have been a small creature. He went back to sleep.

Willie woke up early the next morning, when rain began to fall. Quickly he put on his garbage-bag raincoat. Now he'd stay dry while he waited to be found.

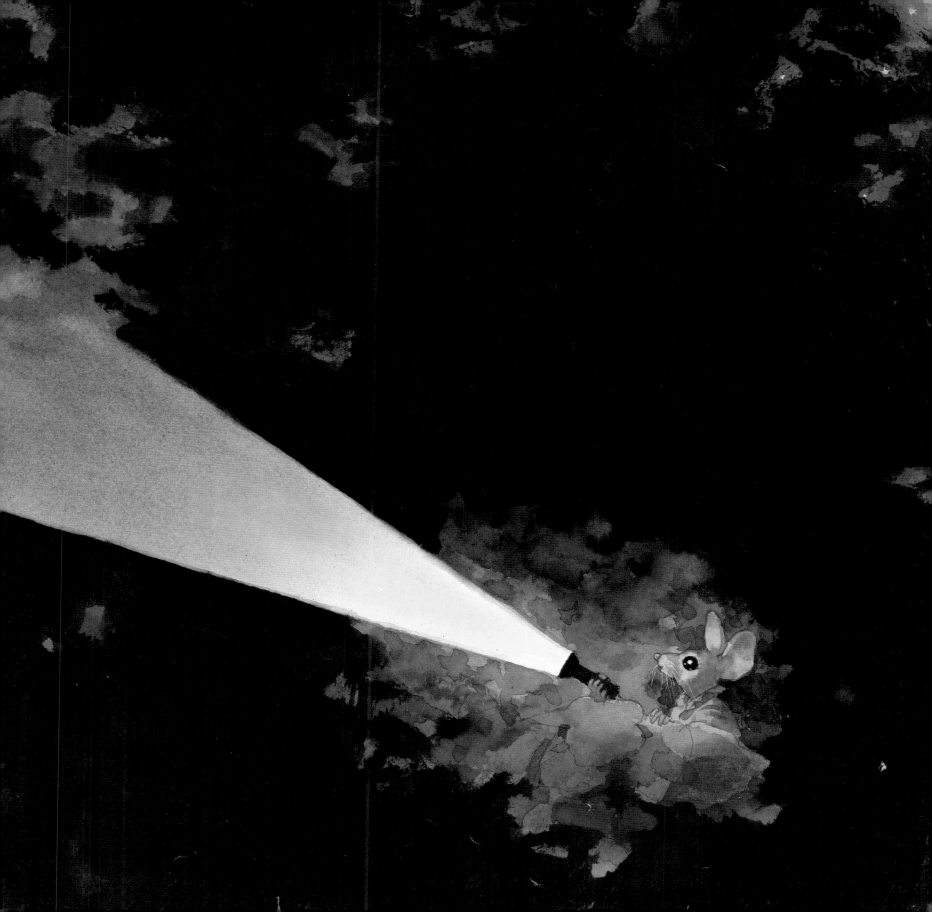

Willie was getting hungry, and he was beginning to think no one would ever find him, when he heard voices calling his name.

"I'm here! I'm here!" Willie shouted, and blew his whistle as hard as he could.

A search party hurried out from behind a heap of car parts. "You all right, Willie?" they asked. "Boy, are we ever glad to see you!"

"Oh, I'm fine," Willie answered. "I just got a little lost, that's all."

The searchers gave Willie a mug of hot chocolate to warm him up, and a jelly sandwich. They offered to carry him on a stretcher, but Willie wanted to walk out on his own.

When Willie saw his parents waiting at the search headquarters he ran to them as fast as he could. He had never been so glad to see his mom and dad in his whole life, and they had never been so glad to see him.

"Thank you! Thank you!" they kept saying to the searchers. "Thank you for finding our son."

"Willie made it easy," the head of the search party explained. "He did everything right, everything a lost hiker should do."

Willie was embarrassed about all the trouble he had caused, but he stood proudly by his parents when he was presented with a search-and-rescue patch to sew on his jacket.

"We're making you an honorary member of our group," the head of the rescue party told Willie. "You are a wilderness-wise hiker."

The whole search party clapped and cheered.

With all these new friends to hike with, Willie knew he'd never take a hike alone again.

AUTHOR'S NOTE

Children sometimes wander away from campsites, stray from their own backyards, or just take off alone on an adventure. Often they have no idea what to do if they find that they are lost.

Willie had been taught what to do. We hope that Willie's experiences in the junkyard will show others how important it is to prepare properly for a hike. Hikers should never set out alone, and if they do get lost, they should do their best to keep dry and warm and try not to panic.

Chances of being found quickly are very good if lost hikers stay where they are when they realize they are lost, and even better if they blow a whistle.

It all worked well for Willie.